Rugby & Rosie

Nan Parson Rossiter

Dutton Children's Books
NEW YORK

Library of Congress Cataloging-in-Publication Data

Rossiter, Nan Parson.
Rugby and Rosie / by Nan Parson Rossiter [author / illustrator].
—1st ed.   p. cm.
Summary: Relates how a family and their dog help prepare
a puppy for training as a guide dog for the blind.
ISBN 0-525-45484-5
[1. Dogs—Training—Fiction.   2. Guide dogs—Fiction.
3. Friendship—Fiction.]   I. Title.
PZ7.R72223Ru   1997
[E]—dc20   96-14688   CIP   AC

Published in the United States 1997 by Dutton Children's Books,
a division of Penguin USA Inc.
375 Hudson Street, New York, New York 10014
Designed by Amy Berniker
Printed in Hong Kong
First Edition
1 3 5 7 9 10 8 6 4 2

For my parents

A heartfelt thank-you to Guiding Eyes for the Blind, Inc.,
in Yorktown Heights, New York, for their research assistance,
and a humble thank-you to the Guiding Hands
that have blessed me so richly

Rugby is my dog. He is a chocolate Labrador, and we have had him for as long as I can remember.

He walks with me to the school-bus stop in the morning, and he meets me there when I get home. He follows me around

when I do my chores, and he sleeps beside my bed at night. He is my best friend.

We used to do everything together—just the two of us.

Then Rosie came.

One fall day, my dad brought home a little yellow puppy. Her name was Rosie. She was so cute that I loved her right away. But she wasn't an ordinary puppy. She was coming to live with my family for only a year. Then Rosie would be old enough to go to a special school. There she would learn how to be a guide dog for a blind person. She and her new owner would always be together. They would be best friends. Just like Rugby and me.

I knew all this before Rosie came, but Rugby didn't. I held the
puppy out to him to see how he would greet Rosie. She leaned
forward eagerly and licked Rugby right on the nose.

Rugby gave one sniff and turned away. He made it very clear he wasn't interested in being friends.

"Come on, Rugby," I said. "She wants to play with you." And it was true. Rosie did want to play. But Rugby wasn't in the mood.

My mom and dad told me to be patient with Rugby, that he'd get used to having another dog around the house. But I wasn't sure. He looked so sad. Maybe he thought I didn't love him anymore, which wasn't true!

Rosie fit in with the family right away. She was so friendly and always wanted to play. She would chase after anything and then run back. She loved everyone in the family—even Rugby! But he still wasn't friendly. Day after day, Rugby just moped around and wouldn't play with us.

That didn't bother Rosie one bit. She thought Rugby was the greatest. She trotted along after him, ran between his legs, tripped him, jumped on him, and barked at him.

Rugby did his best to ignore her.

But Rosie just wouldn't give up.

Then one day, Rugby was not waiting at the school-bus stop. I was worried. He *always* met me at the bus stop.

I ran home—and there I found Rugby asleep on the porch. Curled up in a little ball next to him was Rosie. "Rugby!" I said. They both looked up at me and wagged their tails. Rosie yawned and stretched and settled back down against Rugby's side.

From then on, Rugby and Rosie were always together. They romped and played and chased the falling leaves. And they *both* waited for me at the bus stop.

Rosie was getting bigger. But she was still a puppy with lots of energy. Poor old Rugby tried his best to keep up! Soon winter came, and the three of us were racing and chasing through the new snow. We had so much fun together!

Sometimes it felt as if Rosie had always been with us—and always would be. I didn't want to think about the day when she would have to leave.

Rosie was old enough now for short lessons. Dad showed me how to teach her simple commands: *come, sit, stand, down, stay,* and *heel.*

We all worked to teach her good manners. A dog who begged for food at the table or jumped up on people would not make a good guide dog.

Rosie learned fast. Dad said that she was very smart and loved to please people. But she would have to pass many tests before she could become a guide dog.

I asked Dad what would happen if Rosie didn't pass the tests. He said that she couldn't be a guide dog, but she could still be a good pet. Then we would be able to keep her.

Now I didn't know what to think. I wanted Rosie to do well. I wanted to be proud of her. And I wanted her to help a blind person someday. I knew how important that was. But it was getting harder and harder to think of Rosie going away. And how could I explain it to Rugby? He loved Rosie as much as I did. Now the three of us were best friends.

When spring came, my family started taking Rosie on trips. We wanted her to be used to cars and buses and to the places where she would have to take her blind owner, like the bank and the store. We even took her to a restaurant. Of course, Rugby couldn't come with us. He always looked a little sad when Rosie got to go somewhere he couldn't go. And I knew he would be waiting for us when we got home.

Rosie would jump out of the car, and the two of them would race off, barking and playing and jumping. Later, they would come home in time for dinner, muddy and wet, with their tongues hanging out.

Soon summer came. The days were long and hot. Rosie was almost full grown. She was a beautiful dog. She and Rugby liked to sleep in the cool shade together. Sometimes the three of us

went swimming in a nearby pond. Rugby and Rosie loved to fetch sticks and tennis balls that I threw into the water.

It was a wonderful summer, and I wanted it to last forever.

I knew that when fall came, it would be time for Rosie to go. When that day did come, I tried to be brave. Rugby and I stood and watched as Dad opened the car door for Rosie to jump in. Rugby wasn't upset. He didn't know that Rosie wasn't coming back. But I was so sad. I took Rugby on a long walk and tried not to think about Rosie. It was just like old times, before she came—when there were just the two of us.

When Dad came home, Rugby was waiting, his tail wagging. But, of course, Rosie wasn't in the car. Rugby looked all over for her. He whined. I wanted to explain everything, but I knew he couldn't understand. Instead, I buried my face in his neck and whispered, "She's gone, and I miss her, too."

We all missed Rosie very much, especially Rugby. Her trainers called several times. At first, I hoped that Rosie wasn't doing well. Then she could come back to live with us. But the trainers said that she was doing fine and would graduate with her new owner soon. That made me feel so mixed-up. I didn't want to think about Rosie with a new owner, but I knew how important Rosie would be to a person who needed her. Could that person love her as much as Rugby and I had?

I wanted to go to the graduation and see Rosie again. Then I had a great idea. I asked Dad if we could take Rugby, too. I knew how he'd missed Rosie—after all, they'd been best friends.

We got special permission for Rugby to go to the graduation. I could hardly wait.

At the graduation, there were lots of people and dogs. Rugby spotted Rosie right away. She was in her guide-dog harness, standing beside her new owner. She seemed so calm, and we thought she looked so proud. Rugby bounded over to her, pulling me along. The two dogs greeted each other nose to nose, tails wagging. But Rosie would not leave her owner's side. She was a working dog now with an important job to do.

Her owner talked to us for a while. She told us how grateful she was to have Rosie and what a wonderful dog she was. And she thanked us for taking good care of her while she was a puppy.

When it was time to go, we said good-bye to Rosie. Poor Rugby. On the way home in the car, I tried to make him feel better. I talked to him and patted him. I told him that her new owner loved her and would take good care of her.

The next morning, Rugby was still moping around when my dad left in the car. I was excited—and nervous, too.

I knew where my dad was going.

When the car came back, I was waiting with Rugby. Dad got out. He had a wiggly little puppy in his arms. I knew I was holding on to Rugby too tightly—wishing, hoping. I wanted him to know that, because we had all loved Rosie so much, we had decided we would help raise another puppy that would be ours for a year.

Dad knelt down in front of Rugby. "Rugby," he said, "this is Blue."

And Rugby leaned forward and licked that little puppy right on the nose.

AFTERWORD

Hundreds of families like the one in this book offer temporary homes to carefully bred puppies that have the potential to be guide dogs. For the first year of the puppy's life, the families play a very important role by providing the dog with early lessons in being a guide dog. People who are raising guide-dog puppies lavish them with love and attention and try to expose them to the many kinds of environments they will encounter as working dogs. They ride in cars, trains, and buses; they are led into supermarkets, restaurants, and busy downtown areas. In this way, the puppies learn at a very early age not to be afraid of loud noises or lots of commotion.

After about sixteen to eighteen months, the young dogs leave their temporary families to work for three to four months with a professional trainer at a special guide-dog school. If the dogs pass all the difficult training tests, they are ready to become guide dogs for blind people who need a steady, smart companion and a sharp pair of eyes.

German shepherds, Labrador retrievers, and golden retrievers are the most suitable dogs for guide work. All of these breeds adapt easily to different climates and environments. They are large enough to keep up with walking humans but not too big for small cars or apartments. Their smooth coats are easy to care for. Most important, they are gentle, enjoy human companionship, and are eager to please their owners.

There are several foundations in the United States that breed and train dogs to serve as lifelong teammates and companions to blind people all over the world. The first one was founded in 1929, and since then eleven thousand trained dog guides have been matched with nearly six thousand men and women in the United States and Canada.

There is only one trained guide dog for every hundred blind persons in the United States; less than 2 percent of the blind population uses guide dogs. All fifty states and U.S. territories protect the right of blind people and their dogs to go wherever the public is allowed.

Guide dogs change the lives of the people for whom they work. They allow their owners increased mobility, independence, and self-confidence in ways many of them had never imagined. Morris Frank, the first person to use a guide dog in the United States, once said, "It was glorious—just the dog and a leather strap linking me to life."

To find out more information about guide dogs or to apply for one, please call or write to THE SEEING EYE, INC., P.O. Box 375; Morristown, NJ 07963-0375, (201) 539-4425. Your local library may also have a listing of guide-dog schools in your area.